Artesian **Press**

MW01045127

THE
INDIAN HILLS
HORROR

ANNE SCHRAFF

Artesian **Press**

P.O. Box 355 Buena Park, CA 90621

Take Ten Books
Horror

From the Eye of the Cat	1-58659-071-5
Cassette	1-58659-076-6
The Indian Hills Horror	**1-58659-072-3**
Cassette	**1-58659-077-4**
The Oak Tree Horror	1-58659-073-1
Cassette	1-58659-078-2
The Pack	1-58659-074-X
Cassette	1-58659-079-0
Return to Gallows Hill	1-58659-075-8
Cassette	1-58659-080-4

Other Take Ten Themes:

Mystery
Sports
Adventure
Chillers
Thrillers
Disaster
Fantasy
Romance

Project Editor: Dwayne Epstein
Illustrations: Fujiko
Graphic Design: Tony Amaro
©2001 Artesian Press

www.artesianpress.com

 *Artesian* **Press**   ISBN 1-58659-072-3

CONTENTS

Chapter 1 5

Chapter 2 14

Chapter 3 21

Chapter 4 31

Chapter 5 36

Chapter 6 39

Chapter 7 43

Chapter 8 47

Chapter 9 50

Chapter 10 53

Chapter 1

"Liza!" Mom cried. "Do you know how lucky we are?" Mom had a big smile on her pretty face as she held out her arms and twirled like a dancer. "Did you ever, in your wildest dreams, think we'd live in such a lovely big house?"

Liza Nash was sixteen and had just started her junior year of high school in this new neighborhood. It was very beautiful. The houses were built on full acres of land that were surrounded by rolling hills. Everybody had three cars, and some people had horses, too. There was a big gate welcoming people to this development called Indian Hills.

"Now," Mom said, "you can see why your father and I have been working sixty hours a week in the office. This is our reward!"

All the streets were named after trees growing in the development. Liza and her parents lived on Oak Street.

"Liza, say something," Mom said. "Aren't you excited?"

"I hate my new school, and this house is too big. I wish I was back in our old neighborhood," Liza said. She turned and walked down the hall toward her bedroom.

"Darling," Mom called, hurrying after her. "Just give yourself some time. You'll love it here."

Suddenly, an amazing thing happened. An arrow seemed to come from nowhere, sailed past Liza's head, and drove itself into the wall. Liza grabbed her face and screamed. Dad came running in from the patio, where he was looking at the pool.

Liza was sobbing in her mother's arms when Dad came in. "What's going on?" Dad asked.

"Oh, Ed," Mom said in a shaky

voice. "An arrow almost went through Liza's head. It was such a freak thing!"

"Are you all right, Liza?" Dad asked, grabbing her shoulder.

Liza was still too frightened to talk. Mom answered for her, saying, "She's fine. She was just scared. The arrow seemed to come out of the floor, but that couldn't be. Look Ed, it's stuck in the wall."

Dad walked over to the wall and said, "Someone must have shot this from a bow. I'm telling you Susan, there's no getting away from criminals these days. Even when you pay a lot of money to live in the best neighborhood in town, you're still not safe."

The police arrived twenty minutes later. Two officers came in to take a look at the arrow and talk to the Nashs.

"It's a very old arrow," one of the officers said. "Looks like it came from a museum. Some kids must have stolen it from the Indian museum."

"Where did you say it came from?" the other officer asked.

"It seemed to come from the floor," Mom said, "but that's impossible, isn't it?"

"And then it came at my head and just missed me," Liza added. She was calmer now, but her voice was still shaky.

The two officers crawled around the floor until one said, "Here. Something ripped through the floor and the rug."

He seemed very puzzled as he took pictures of the floor and wall. They carefully pulled the arrow out of the wall and then promised to look into the strange event.

After the police left, Dad shook his head. "How could the arrow come through the floor? We don't have a basement. It doesn't make sense," he said.

"I wish we hadn't come here," Liza said. "Our old house was better, and

8

all my friends lived nearby. I loved Jefferson High. Everybody at Indian Hills High has a lot of money and isn't very friendly."

"There is nothing bad about having money," Dad said. "Stop complaining, Liza. How about being grateful for what you've got instead of complaining all the time? How about that nice little car you have in the garage?"

"It's not about the car," Liza said.

"Of course not," Dad said. "You just want everything to be the way you want it. You can make new friends. Your brother has already made some nice new friends."

Liza wasn't sure how she felt, but she knew she wasn't happy. She felt bad long before the arrow almost hit her. She just didn't feel at home in Indian Hills. She didn't think she ever would.

When Ken, Liza's fourteen-year-old brother came home, he shouted,

"What's all the excitement? I just saw cops leaving."

Ken and Liza were very different. As long as he could play sports, Ken was happy anywhere. Liza was shy, and it was much harder for her to make friends.

"Some troublemaker shot an arrow into our house and it hit the wall. It gave Liza a real scare," Dad said.

"Wow!" Ken said. "Do you think they meant to shoot at us?"

"No," Mom said. "There's probably an archery range somewhere near here and the arrow missed the target."

"It was an old arrow," Liza said, "like the kind used a real long time ago. It seemed to come out of our floor!"

"Wow!" Ken said. "Maybe some of the Indians who used to live around here came back."

"Don't be ridiculous," Dad said. "There probably never were Indians around here. And if there were, they've been gone for a hundred years. It was just a freak accident."

"Yeah," Ken agreed. "Anyway, I'm going to try out for the football team at school next season. The coach thinks I have a good chance."

"Great!" Dad said, smiling. "That's terrific, Ken."

Liza went outside and got on her bike. Indian Hills did have nice bike trails in the development. One worked its way around a small lake where ducks floated peacefully. Liza always rode her bike whenever she was unhappy. Now she rode toward the lake.

The sun had gone down and the hills were covered in the mist of twilight. Before Liza left the house, Mom had called after her, "Now don't be late for dinner. Rosie is making Italian pepper steak and you like that."

Rosie was the family cook and

housekeeper. The Nashs hired Rosie even before they moved to Indian Hills. Since both Mom and Dad worked ten hours a day, Mom had no time for housework. Rosie did the cleaning and cooking during the week, then she went home on weekends.

Liza looked over the development of lovely three-level homes. She remembered when her family didn't have much money. When Liza was six and her brother was four, they lived in a much smaller house in a nice neighborhood. Then, Mom and Dad worked many extra hours over the next few years. They also made money in the stock market. They could now afford to live in Indian Hills.

When Liza was growing up, she saw Rosie more than she did her own mother. Rosie was a fifty-year-old grandmother when she came to work for Liza's family. When Liza remembered bumps and bruises from falling off her bike, it was Rosie who held her while she cried. When it was time for a bedtime story, it was Rosie who told it with her Mexican accent.

Liza rode her bike to the edge of the lake and stared out over the peaceful water. It looked like a mirror, getting darker as the sun went down.

"Who are you?" said a male voice behind Liza.

Liza froze in fear. She turned to see a young man in jeans and no shirt. He looked angry. His dark eyes seem to glow with fury.

Chapter 2

"My family lives here," Liza said nervously. "We just moved here."

"Oh, one of *them*!" the young man said with a frown. He had black hair and dark skin.

"Michael," an older man called to him. "I need your help with this light fixture."

The young man turned quickly and walked away. The older man walked toward Liza, who was getting on her bike. "Excuse my son," he said. "We take care of the grounds and do repairs here. My son has a bad attitude and sometimes he is rude."

"It's okay," Liza said. "He just scared me a little." She rode away as the two men worked on a streetlight. All the streetlights in Indian Hills were made to look like old-fashioned

14

lanterns. Everything in Indian Hills was made to look fancy.

Liza pedaled down Oak Street toward home. She didn't know any of the neighbors and wasn't sure she wanted to know them. Everybody lived behind huge lawns and high brick walls.

As Liza passed a house 200 feet from where she lived, she saw a man and a woman in the driveway, shouting excitedly. The new car in the driveway seemed lopsided, as if it had flat tires.

"You must have let the sprinklers run too long," the man yelled at his wife. "You made the whole yard a soggy mess. That's why the driveway is sinking!"

"I didn't do anything," the woman yelled. "The gardener takes care of the lawn!"

"Look at the tires," the man cried. "They're sunk into the cement!"

"I'll call a tow truck," the woman

"Look at the tires," the man cried. "They're sunk into the cement!"

said with a panicky voice.

"A tow truck!" the man yelled. "What good is that? By the time it gets here, the car will be gone! I've got to try to drive it out of the hole." He jumped into the car and pushed down hard on the gas pedal, trying to drive out of the sinking driveway.

Liza watched the scene with horror. She never saw anything like it. The driveway seemed to be swallowing the car. The wheels had sunk up to the hubcaps.

"Harold, get out of that thing!" the man's wife screamed. The man continued to push on the gas pedal, trying to save his car. It was as if it were being sucked into quicksand.

The woman screamed again. Then, she turned and ran back to the house. Within minutes, fire engines and police cars came racing up the street as the car sank to its fenders. It took several firemen, using their equipment, to save the man. As they worked, the car kept sinking.

About two dozen of the neighbors came out to watch what was happening under the searchlights. One woman cried, "Look, it's almost gone! What is going on?"

Liza watched the ground seem to "eat" the car until she saw nothing but the roof. Other fire engines arrived as the police put ropes around the area.

Liza's mother came down the street to see what all the excitement was about. "What is it, Liza?" she called when she spotted her daughter. "Was there an accident?"

Liza walked her bike quickly toward her mother. "Oh, Mom, there's a big sinkhole in that driveway and it just swallowed up a big car. It was like watching a horror movie!" she said.

"Oh, my," Mom said. "I've heard of sinkholes in places like Florida, where there are swamps under the ground.

What could have caused this?"

"That fool gardener," Harold was shouting. "I knew the sprinklers were on too long. The ground got too soggy. I'm going to take him to court for this!"

As the Nashs ate their dinner that night, Ken said, "Wow, we've just been here a few days and look what's happened already! Somebody shot an arrow at us and now a neighbor almost gets eaten by his driveway. Maybe we picked the wrong neighborhood."

"Nonsense," Dad said. "This is a great neighborhood. The sinkhole down the street is probably the only one in the neighborhood. It has nothing to do with us."

"How do you know, Dad?" Liza asked. "Maybe the builders made a big mistake in the whole development. We could all fall into horrible sinkholes and be buried alive!"

"Oh, Liza," Mother laughed. "You make such a big deal out of everything.

Does anybody want more rolls?"

Liza had tried to make some friends in school that day, but most of the other kids acted a lot cooler than Liza. They all seemed to know the right way to dress and the best CDs to listen to.

One girl, Claudia, had smiled at Liza and said, "Oh, I haven't seen anybody wearing those jeans since grade school."

Before she went to bed that night, Liza told her mother, "I have to get some different clothes." Mom was talking to Dad about stocks and didn't even hear what Liza said.

Suddenly, Liza heard a strange squeak. A groan came from deep within the walls of the house. Their last house often made noises, too. Rosie always smiled and said, "Ah, the house is settling. It's nothing."

This was different. Liza had seen the sinkhole swallow the car down the street. Maybe there was a sinkhole under their house, too.

Chapter 3

Liza didn't sleep well that night. She kept thinking about the sinkhole. When she did sleep, she had nightmares about going to school with all those strangers.

It was a lot easier for Ken because he was a freshman. All the freshmen were new. Liza was a junior. By the time a student is a junior, everybody has picked the people they like because they've already been together for two years. It was hard for new kids like Liza to become part of a group.

The next morning, Liza thought about school as she ate her breakfast. "Maybe I could talk about the sinkhole. I saw the driveway swallow up the car. Maybe the kids will be so interested, they'll talk to me."

Mom and Dad had already gone to

work since they both had a long way to go. Dad drove 60 miles to work and Mom drove 40 miles. Dad would say, "To come home to Indian Hills is worth another hour on the freeway." Mom agreed. They usually got home around eight o'clock each evening.

Rosie took care of everything just fine. Rosie Porales had lived a very hard life as a child in Mexico. She was proud of keeping house and cooking for the Nash family. Rosie also loved the children. She had practically raised Liza and Ken.

"You want more pancakes, Kenny?" Rosie asked. Rosie had come to America when she was twelve. She married a man who was also from Mexico, and they had a hard life raising their children. Then Rosie's husband died. Her children were doing well now, though, and she did not worry about them. She had a little apartment of her own for the weekends, and life was good.

"I'm full, Rosie," Ken said. "Your pancakes are so good!"

"You are a growing boy," Rosie scolded. "You need to eat alot of good food. Look how skinny your brother is, Liza. You are skinny, too."

Liza loved her parents, but sometimes it felt like Rosie was her real mother. Rosie was always there for her. It seemed Mom never was.

"I hate going to my new school, Rosie," Liza said. "Nobody is friendly to me."

"You smile nice and say 'hello' to everybody and you will get some nice friends. Just keep on trying, and somebody will be your friend. It was hard for me and my Carlos when we were young. It was hard for our children, too. If you try and try, pretty soon you'll have nice friends."

Liza drove her car to school even though it was only 2 miles to Indian

Hills High. Almost all the kids drove or were dropped off by their parents.

Ken usually rode with Liza except when Rosie dropped him off. "This is a really cool car," Ken told Liza. "When I get my license though, I want a pickup truck."

"Ken, did you hear all that squeaking and cracking in the house last night?" Liza asked her brother. "It really made me nervous."

"Nah, I had my earphones on and I was playing my new CD."

"I hope there aren't any more sinkholes in the neighborhood," Liza said. "I keep thinking about that car sinking into the driveway."

"I wish I'd seen it," Ken said. "Hey, maybe long ago this was a city dump and they didn't pack down the garbage too good. I read about that happening somewhere and they built houses on it. Pretty soon, the foundations started cracking and the houses broke up."

24

It was hard to imagine that this beautiful valley, surrounded by pretty hills, could ever have been a dump. Liza was curious, though. "I wonder if there's a book about the history of this area," she said.

As they reached Indian Hills High, Ken noticed two pretty girls dressed in cheerleader uniforms. "Wow! They sure are pretty!" he said.

Liza went to her usual classes and did what Rosie said, smiling and saying hello every chance she got. The other girls looked at her as if she were weird. As usual, Liza didn't go to the cafeteria. She ate her lunch alone under the trees. Then she went to the library.

"I'm looking for a book on the history of this area," Liza said.

"Oh yes, we have a wonderful book like that," the librarian said. She quickly brought back a book called *The Battle of Bloody Hills*. She told Liza, "You'll enjoy this."

Liza found a quiet corner in the library and began looking through the book. She read that in the 1700s, a number of Native Americans lived in the area. They fished from nearby streams and ate the pine nuts from the thick forests that grew there at the time. The people planted and harvested wild oats and hunted animals in the hills. It seemed like a very pleasant life.

In the mid-1850s, a wagon train came through and there was a fight between the immigrants and the local Modoc Indians. Seven white men were killed and the U.S. Cavalry came in to make all the Modoc families leave the valley. Most of those who lived through the fight ended up on a reservation far away in Oklahoma Territory.

Liza looked at all the maps in the book but she couldn't find exactly where Indian Hills was built. She took the book back to the librarian. "I live

Liza found a quiet corner in the library to read about the battle of Bloody Hills.

in Indian Hills, and I'd like to know where that is on this old map," she said.

The librarian smiled happily, delighted to find a teenager interested in the history of the area. "Look here, dear. Do you see the area marked Bloody Hills?" she said.

"Yes," Liza said, following the librarian's finger across the page.

"Well, that is where the U.S. Cavalry caught up with the group of rebellious Modocs who had attacked the wagon train. That's why it was known as Bloody Hills. About a hundred men died in the battle, mostly Modocs. The dead cavalrymen were carried away by the other soldiers, of course, and were given a military burial. The Modocs were buried right where they fell.

"Well, for a long time the land just lay there. Then about twelve years ago, a developer bought the land and put a beautiful development in now called

Indian Hills. If you live there, my dear, you're a very lucky girl."

Liza asked the librarian, "Then where we live used to be called Bloody Hills? All those Modocs are buried there?" She had a funny feeling in the pit of her stomach.

"Yes," the librarian said calmly. "That's just an interesting piece of history, dear. Actually, the site where our brave cavalrymen defended the land against the Modocs is rich in historical importance."

"But all those Modocs are buried under the ground where we live," Liza said. Her mouth was going dry.

The librarian frowned. "Dear, it all happened so very long ago," she said.

Trying to smile, Liza checked out the book so she could read it at home. She remembered another history book she had read when she was in fifth grade. In it, the author talked about another battlefield where many had fallen.

"This land is haunted by the spirits of the fallen" that book had said. "Do not walk upon the bones of the brave who fell defending their way of life."

Liza felt sad and a little afraid. Indian Hills was built on a battlefield's graveyard. It was not really Indian Hills. It was Bloody Hills. Everyday, the people who now lived there, walked on the bones of the dead.

Chapter 4

Claudia Kent, who had been rude to Liza in the past, walked over as Liza left the library. "Hi, Liza," she said. "That tank top looks good on you."

Liza had worn the tank top before but nobody had said anything. "Oh, thanks," Liza said.

"A couple of us are going to the mall after school," Claudia said. "Would you like to go?"

Liza's heart jumped. She had just been asked to join one of the coolest groups in school. She couldn't believe she would be hanging out with Claudia, Sherelle, and Mari. "Oh, that would be fun," Liza said. "I've never been to the mall around here."

"Okay," Claudia said. "We can meet at your car. Would you mind driving? I mean, me and Sherelle are sort of grounded. We got a couple of tickets and Mari's car is in the garage."

"Sure, I can drive," Liza said.

After Claudia left, Liza was excited about going to the mall with friends. The rest of the afternoon seemed to go by quickly. She called Rosie and said she'd be coming home late. "Me and some friends are going to the mall."

"See?" Rosie said. "You have some friends already!"

"Yeah," Liza said, giggling. "You were right, Rosie. You're always right!"

After the last class ended, Liza rushed to the parking lot to wait for the other three girls. Claudia was already there. She was tall and slender with long legs. Sherelle was almost as pretty with her huge, dark eyes. Mari was petite and bubbly.

"Is this car new?" Claudia asked.

"Yeah," Liza said. "Dad got it a couple of months ago."

"Nice!" Sherelle said.

As Liza drove to the mall, she told the girls about the sinkhole. "I saw it happen. It was right on our street," she said.

"I heard about that," said Sherelle. "I'm glad we live way over on Birch Street."

"I found something weird in a book today," Liza said. "About a hundred and fifty years ago, our area was called Bloody Hills because of a big battle here between the cavalry and the Modocs. A lot of Modocs are buried right under us."

"That's pretty spooky," Claudia said. "We're living on a cemetery!"

"Yeah, the other day, somebody shot an arrow into our house," Liza said. She was glad she had something interesting to say to her new friends.

"Really?" Mari giggled. "Maybe the dead Indians are getting back at us."

They parked at the mall and the four girls walked down the wide aisle between the stores. Liza's new friends rushed to a stand that had new jewelry.

"I just love jewelry," Claudia said. "Especially these little bracelets."

"Me, too," Sherelle said. "I love those beads. I can't get enough of them."

One woman was in charge of the stand. The gold and silver chains were around the other side.

"Liza, ask the lady if she's got any long gold chains, about 17 inches," Claudia said.

Liza went to the other side of the stand and the woman showed her a few gold chains. Liza liked one chain and bought it for her mother's birthday, which was next month. Then the four girls walked away from the stand.

"What did you get, Liza?" Claudia asked.

Liza held up the chain. "My Mom will like this for her birthday. She always wears gold jewelry," she, said.

"I got it at a good price, too."

"That's cool," Claudia said.

"Let's get some frozen yogurt and look at the stuff we got," Sherelle said.

As the four girls found a table near the yogurt stand, Liza was puzzled by what Sherelle said. Liza bought the gold chain, but the other girls hadn't bought anything.

After the girls got their yogurt, Mari pulled a pair of earrings from her purse. "Aren't they beautiful?" she asked.

Liza stared at the earrings. She had seen them at the stand, but she had not seen Mari buy anything.

Suddenly, Liza became angry. She began to understand why the three girls asked her to keep the clerk busy at the other side of the stand.

Chapter 5

The three girls were giggling as they showed each other their jewelry. "I got a string of beads," Sherelle said, holding it up in the sunlight.

"You stole those things!" Liza said suddenly. She realized that they had used her as a decoy and had planned it all out.

"Oh, those stores have so much," Claudia said. "They know kids take stuff. Besides, it's not like these are expensive diamonds or something. Don't be such a jerk, Liza. All the kids do it. If you want to be stupid and pay, that's your business. What we do is our business."

"You used me," Liza said. "You told me to keep the lady busy so you could steal that stuff. I feel like such a fool."

"Oh, shut up, Liza," Sherelle said.

On the drive back to Indian Hills, Claudia said, "You know, Liza, you really spoiled things today. We were all trying to have some fun, and you acted like we were criminals just because we took some cheap junk."

"I paid thirty dollars for my Mom's gold chain," Liza said. "It wasn't cheap junk, and the stuff you took wasn't junk, either."

"Stop picking on us," Mari said to Liza. "Do you think you're so perfect?"

"I'm not perfect," Liza said. "It's just that stealing is wrong!"

"We don't like being preached to, okay?" Sherelle said. "We've been taking stuff since we were kids, and it doesn't bother anybody. It's like a scavenger hunt."

"It's still stealing," Liza repeated. "People go to jail for stealing."

"Look," Claudia said in a mean voice. "If you say anything about what we did, we'll all say you took stuff, too, get it? It's three against one!"

Liza dropped the three girls off at their houses and drove away. She didn't start crying until they were gone. She would have hated it if they had seen her cry.

Liza understood now. The only reason the three girls asked her to join them at the mall was because she had a car. Once they got to the mall, they didn't want her around. They needed her to keep the clerk busy so they could steal.

It had all been a mean trick. They were never Liza's friends, and they never could be. Liza was alone again, and she felt worse than before.

Chapter 6

When Liza turned into the family's driveway, she saw the dark young man who had scared her earlier. He was trimming the hedges in the common area in the middle of the street.

"Hi," Liza said, hoping to make a friend.

"Hi," he said. He seemed to be in a better mood now.

"I don't mean to be rude or anything," Liza said, "but you don't live around here, do you?"

He stopped trimming the bush. "No, I live about 30 miles from here. My father and I are part of the landscaping crew, but my forefathers lived here."

"You're a Modoc Indian, aren't you?" Liza asked.

"Yes," he said. His eyes opened

wide in surprise. "How did you know that?"

"I read a book about the local history. You probably know about Bloody Hills, don't you?" Liza asked.

"Yes, I do, but I didn't read it in a book. I heard it from my father and his father," the young man said.

"My name is Liza Nash," she said, hoping he'd give his name, too.

"Michael is my name," he said. "Mike."

"Do you know about the sinkhole that swallowed the car?" Liza asked him.

"Yeah," he said.

"I hope it doesn't happen anymore. It was scary," Liza said.

"I just wouldn't live here," Mike said, turning and starting his clipping again. Liza still stood there. After a few moments, Mike stopped and looked at her. His dark eyes looked angry.

"Liza, do you have a grandparent

who died?" he asked.

"My grandfather died when I was ten. I loved him a lot." Liza said.

"Where is he buried?" Mike asked.

"In Mystic Hills. It's a beautiful memorial park. We go there sometimes and leave flowers in the little vase by his grave marker," Liza said.

"Suppose someday a housing development is built in Mystic Hills," Mike said. His voice shook with anger. "Maybe they will cover up the markers and make golf courses."

Liza was horrified. "No! They never build houses where people are buried," she said.

"They did it here," Mike said. "A lot of my forefathers are buried under these pretty houses."

Liza thought of the lines in that old history book: "This land is haunted by the spirits of the fallen. Do not walk upon the bones of the brave who fell defending their way of life."

Liza was so upset that she didn't hear the strange, cracking sound of the huge oak tree branch above her head. Mike's eyes opened wide and he ran at Liza. He grabbed her and threw her into a small, grassy ditch.

It all happened so fast, Liza did not even know what was going on. For a terrible moment, she thought Mike was attacking her in anger.

Liza then saw the huge tree tremble and crash. The ground under the oak tree gave way, weakened by another sinkhole. The tree fell to the ground on the spot where Liza had been standing a second earlier.

Chapter 7

When Liza realized what had happened, she jumped up from the ditch and grabbed Mike's hand. "You saved my life!" she cried.

"Luckily, I saw it coming," Mike said. "You okay?"

Before she could answer, other people came running to see what had happened. They had heard the loud sound of the tree falling. One of them was Rosie, her eyes wide with fear. "Are you okay? Were you close to the tree when it fell?" Rosie asked, giving Liza a big hug.

"Yeah, I was right there when Mike . . ." Liza turned to look for Mike, but he left before the others arrived.

Some of the homeowners at Indian Hills were now talking about a lawsuit. "If this whole development has been built on unstable ground, then the builders are going to see us in court," one man shouted.

Liza didn't think it was built on unstable ground. She was afraid it was built on *haunted* ground.

Liza saw Mike in the distance, leaning against his pickup truck. She hurried to catch him before he drove away.

"Mike," Liza called to him. "You're a hero. Why did you run away?"

"No, I'm not," Mike said angrily. "Don't tell anybody what happened. I just gave you a shove out of the way. Anybody else would have done the same."

"What's going on around here, Mike?" Liza asked him. "Do you know what's going on?"

Mike didn't say anything for a few minutes. Then, when he began speaking, it was not directly to Liza. It was as if he were talking to no one in particular and also to everybody.

"The men who died here need to be honored," he said quietly. "There must be at least a monument or marker. Seventy-seven brave Modocs lie buried under these houses and there is no monument. There is no place where a person could go to pray or to pay respects."

Liza turned and walked slowly back to her house. Mom was home and was excited about a new company whose stock had tripled.

"Mom, I have to talk to you," Liza said.

"Is something wrong at school?" Mom asked.

"No," Liza said. "It's about another one of those sinkholes. A big oak tree fell today, Mom," Liza said.

"Well, we better get those engineers here to find what the problem is," Mom said. "It's terrible that we paid such a high price to live here, and now we have these awful problems."

Liza told her mother about what had happened at Bloody Hills. She told her mother about the Modocs buried under Indian Hills. She said a Modoc in the area believes there should be a monument honoring the dead.

"What would it hurt to put up a monument to show a little respect? Nobody would build a housing development over one of our cemeteries," Liza said.

"Sweetheart, don't be silly!" Mom said. She started to laugh. "Oh, you're making a joke, right? Well, I'm too tired for jokes. Right after dinner, I've got to get on the computer and work on some numbers."

Liza turned and walked outside. She waited for her father to come home. Unfortunately, she didn't have much hope that Dad would listen, either.

Chapter 8

Liza decided to wait until later to talk to her father. He usually took a walk around the neighborhood after dinner as part of his plan to stay healthy. Tonight Liza went with him.

Dad started talking about a man at his office who wasn't doing his job well. "I may have to fire him," he said.

Liza then told her father about Bloody Hills. She said she had met a Modoc man who told her the troubles at Indian Hills were because of the unhappy spirits of the dead Modocs.

"What kind of nonsense is that?" Dad asked. "I never heard anything so stupid."

"Dad, that oak tree that got weak because of a new sinkhole, almost fell on me today," Liza said.

Dad stopped and turned, grabbing

Liza's shoulders. "What?" he cried.

"Mike, the Modoc man, pushed me out of the way, Dad. He said it's dangerous here. I don't want to stay here any longer. I'm scared!" Liza said.

"Honey, it's just a mistake the builder made," Dad said. "All kinds of experts will be coming in to fix things. It's okay, sweetheart."

"What would be wrong with putting up a historical marker? It would show a little respect for the men who are buried here. The Modoc man said that would help. It wouldn't cost much," Liza said.

"Do you think I'm going to tell all the homeowners that I think we need a historical marker honoring some dead Indians so the earth stops moving around here?" Dad asked. "Do you expect me to make such a fool of myself?"

"You could just say it's a marker where people could sometimes leave flowers, like we do for Grandpa." Liza said.

"Liza, we go to the cemetery to leave flowers for Grandpa. This is a housing development," Dad said.

"No, it's also a cemetery," Liza said. She turned away from her father so he wouldn't see her tears. "Just forget it. I shouldn't even have said anything!"

Angrily, Liza said, "You know what? The only real father I ever had was Grandpa. And the only real mother I have is Rosie." Liza began to run and jogged home ahead of her father.

It was the first time Liza came right out and told her father what she had been feeling for years. All her parents really cared about were their jobs and making money. They said the money would give their children a good life. Liza didn't feel like she was having a good life.

Chapter 9

Before Liza went to sleep that night, she saw her father standing in the doorway of her room. "Sweetheart, may I come in?" he asked softly.

"I guess so," Liza said.

"At the homeowners meeting on Friday, I'll ask them about building the historical marker. They'll probably all laugh, but I will do it," Dad said.

Liza sat up in bed. "Thanks, Dad."

On Friday night, Liza went to the meeting with her father. Most of the people there were angry. The man who came to speak for the builder kept pulling on at his collar as if he were very hot.

Liza leaned over to her father and whispered, "Just tell them this was called Bloody Hills and tell them why."

Dad nodded. He looked very

unhappy. The last thing he wanted to do was talk about a marker honoring the Modocs, but he got up, cleared his throat, and talked about Bloody Hills. He talked about the seventy-seven men buried under the houses and said there should be a marker out of respect. There was whispering around the room.

"What has that got to do with our crumbling houses?" asked Bob Kent, Claudia's father.

"Maybe nothing," Dad said. "However, if we built our homes on top of a Modoc cemetery, we should at least respect them with a historical marker."

A woman in a fur coat began to laugh. "Oh, I get it. Mr. Nash is trying to say the angry spirits of the Modocs are moving the ground under our homes," she said.

Liza jumped up and shouted over the laughter, "What would be so wrong with putting up a historical marker?"

"We're not here to honor the dead," Mr. Kent shouted. "I don't care if a thousand Indians are buried here! We're here to make sure our houses don't fall into sinkholes!"

The suggestion for the marker didn't get anywhere. The meeting fell apart, as homeowners screamed about lawsuits. The builder's man escaped through a side door.

"Thanks for trying, Dad," Liza said as they went home. "It meant a lot to me."

Around midnight, the sounds of fire engines woke the Nashs. The family looked out their front window.

"What happened?" Mom asked.

"The house across the street," Liza gasped. "I don't see it anymore."

"That's impossible!" Mom cried.

Dad put his arm around Mom's shoulders. "No," he said. "The house where the Gleesons lived is not there anymore."

Chapter 10

The police put a rope around the huge sinkhole that had swallowed the Gleesons' home. Luckily, the family was away visiting relatives. By the time they got home, engineers, safety, and soil experts were all over the place.

Liza didn't go to school that day. She rode her bike through the development until she found Mike. "Mike, did you hear about the house that disappeared last night?" she said.

After he nodded, Liza asked, "Mike, could you maybe make a historical marker telling about Bloody Hills and the people buried here?"

Mike was silent for a few minutes. He finally said, "I could. It would be just a wooden marker."

"Make it, Mike," Liza said. "Make it quickly."

Liza met Mike on Friday night. He and his father carried the marker in their pickup truck. Liza led them to the entrance to Indian Hills, near the large gate. Mike and his father dug deep holes then put in two redwood posts. They nailed up the marker that read: *This land was home to the Modoc people. In November 1863, after a battle between white immigrants and Modocs, the U.S. Cavalry attacked the Modoc people. Eighteen cavalrymen and seventy-seven Modoc warriors died in a battle, causing this land to be called Bloody Hills. This land is the burial place for seventy-seven Modocs and is sacred ground.*

From out of the darkness came Bob Kent and two other homeowners. Mr. Kent stared at the marker and shouted, "That stupid marker ruins the whole entrance."

"Leave it alone," Liza said.

Mr. Kent said angrily, "I didn't pay all that money for my house so such an ugly thing could be at the entrance."

As Mr. Kent and the other two men walked toward the wooden marker, the sound of chanting mourners filled the air. Liza turned to see Mike and his father. Their faces were smeared with wet paste and ashes as they danced in a slow circle around the marker. At first, Liza thought the chants were coming from them.

The sounds of chanting grew louder and louder. They seemed to come from a hundred and then a thousand voices. The sound grew and grew until the night was filled with wailing.

Liza looked into the darkness and saw people from Indian Hills, including her own family, slowly walking toward the marker to see what it was all about. There was no laughter like there had been at the meeting.

Mr. Kent and the other two men backed away from the marker with looks of terror on their faces.

There were strange, terrifying sounds that no one had ever heard before. They were screams of pain and shouts of triumph--wild, savage sounds from a time long past.

Mr. Kent and the others walked slowly away as the night became quiet

Liza and her family suddenly heard screams of pain and shouts of triumph from a time long past.

again. Mike and his father drove away in their truck. Liza's family stood back as Liza knelt down near the marker. She whispered, "Rest in peace," as she did so often at her grandfather's grave. She then walked to where her parents and brother waited. They all walked slowly home.

Liza heard crickets singing in the night. She had never before heard crickets singing at Indian Hills.

The engineers and the soil experts continued to search for the cause of the terrible sinkholes. They held meetings and continued their search for the answer to what happened.

Liza was sure the strange events were over, though. Maybe someday soon she would even like living there.